# I See Something GRAND

by Mitzi Chandler

Illustrated by Barbara Epstein-Eagle

GRAND CANYON ASSOCIATION

*This book is dedicated to my grandchildren and to the memory of Karen L. Taylor.*
*Thank you Miss Kelsey Ann Fekkes for giving me the idea for this book.*
*— Mitzi Chandler*

*I dedicate the drawings in this book to the memory of my grandma, Ester Israel Bernstein,*
*who taught me about love, acceptance, beauty, and chicken soup.*
*— Barbara Epstein-Eagle*

Copyright © 1994 by Grand Canyon Association
Post Office Box 399, Grand Canyon Arizona 86023
Illustrations © 1994 by Barbara Epstein-Eagle
Printed on recycled paper in Hong Kong

ISBN 0-938216-50-3
LCN 94-075653

Designed by Diane Goldsmith
Square Moon Productions
Orinda, CA 94563

"Are we almost there, Grandpa?" Kelsey asked.

"Yes, Kelsey," her grandfather answered.
"The Grand Canyon is just beyond those trees."

"Look, Kelsey!" he exclaimed.
"There's the Grand Canyon!"

"Wow!" Kelsey cried. "We're really high!
It makes butterflies in my tummy.

Hold my hand, Grandpa."

Her grandfather smiled and took her hand.
"Yes, the bottom is very far down.
The Canyon is about one mile deep," he explained.

"What does GRAND mean?" Kelsey asked.

"It means something is SPECIAL," her grandfather said.
"The Grand Canyon is very big and very old.
There is no other place like it on earth.
Look, Kelsey, the Canyon stretches as far as we can see."

"Is the Canyon *this* long?" Kelsey asked her grandfather,
stretching as far as she could stretch.

He chuckled. "It's longer than that, Kelsey.
It's hundreds of miles long."

"Then it's really, REALLY long!" she shouted.

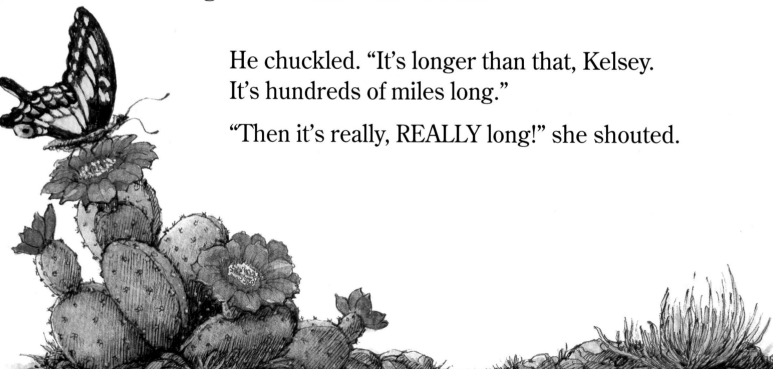

Then Kelsey asked quietly,
"Grandpa, is the Canyon as old as you?"

"Oh, it's much older than me," he answered.
"It's as old as *all* the Grandpas that ever lived."

"Wow!" she exclaimed.
"That's really, really, REALLY old."

Kelsey was curious.
"How did it get here?" she asked.
"Did people dig the Grand Canyon?"

"No, Kelsey," her grandfather told her.
"A long time ago the Colorado River carved
out the Grand Canyon. And each time it
rains, water runs down the canyon walls
and washes tiny pieces of rock and sand
with it.

It's called 'erosion'."

"E-ro-sion," Kelsey repeated.
"That's a big word, Grandpa."

"Yes it is," her Grandpa continued.
"Erosion also happens when the river
at the bottom wooshes between the
canyon walls and washes sand
and rock into the river."

"Is erosion happening now?"
Kelsey asked.

"Yes," her grandfather said.
"The Grand Canyon is getting wider
and deeper all the time."

"Look, Grandpa," Kelsey laughed.
"The Grand Canyon is growing DOWN
and I am growing UP."

"What animals live at the Grand Canyon?" she asked.

"Well," her grandfather said, "this morning
we saw some deer eating leaves."

"They have long ears, Grandpa," she remembered.

"That's right, Kelsey," he said proudly.

"We watched an Abert squirrel climb a tree," her Grandfather told her.

"We watched ravens soar over the Canyon," he continued. "We saw a chipmunk scamper over rocks."

"He ran fast to his hiding place, Grandpa," Kelsey whispered.

"Yes, he did," her grandfather agreed.

"And remember, Grandpa," Kelsey laughed, "we sat on a bench and watched a rock squirrel eating a pine nut."

"Yes," her grandfather chuckled. "Other animals live at the Canyon too, but we probably won't see them today, Kelsey. I'll tell you about some of them."

"Bighorn sheep live on steep cliffs."

"Coyotes call to each other by howling."

"Bobcats usually sleep
in rocky dens."

"Collared lizards sun themselves on warm rocks."

"Pink rattlesnakes curl up in rocks at the bottom of the Canyon."

"Scorpions have a stinger
at the end of their tail."

"Elk are the biggest animals living at the Grand Canyon."

"Lots and lots of animals live at the Grand Canyon, don't they, Grandpa?" Kelsey asked.

"Yes they do, Kelsey," her grandfather answered.

"And lots and lots of people from all over the world come to visit the Grand Canyon because it is such a SPECIAL place," he continued.

"Grandpa," Kelsey said suddenly.
"*You* have the same first name as the Grand Canyon.
You are my GRAND father and you are SPECIAL!"

"Thank you, Kelsey," he laughed. "And did you know that *you* have the same first name as the Grand Canyon?"

"I do?" she said, surprised.

"Yes," he said. "You are my GRAND daughter and you are very SPECIAL."

"I know, Grandpa," she said, giving him a big hug. "I want to come back when I'm bigger and learn more about the Grand Canyon," Kelsey decided.

"We'll come back when you are big enough to hike down to the bottom," her grandfather promised. "Would you like to do that, Kelsey?"

"Oh, yes!" she said, taking his hand in hers. "That would be just GRAND, Grandpa."